The Wind ~in the~ Willows ANNUAL · 1986

Compiled and written by Angus P Allan
and illustrated by Michael Noble.
Editorial Direction by Colin Shelbourn and Terry Tatnell.
Art Direction and design by John Bickerton and Mik Baines.
Based on the characters created by Kenneth Grahame
and the networked ITV series produced by
Cosgrove Hall Productions Ltd. ©
Series scripts by Rosemary Anne Sisson.
Printed and bound by Purnell and Sons (Book Production) Ltd,
Paulton, Bristol. Member of BPCC plc.
Published in Great Britain by
Independent Television Publications Ltd
for Independent Television Books Ltd,
247 Tottenham Court Road, London, WIP 0AU.
ISBN 0 907965 40 7

Here are two messages in which pictures are used instead of words. As you can see, sometimes letters have been added or taken away from them. Can you work out what they mean? In case you'd like to know, this kind of picture-code is very old indeed, and is called a 'rebus' which is Latin and means 'from things'!

BEAUTIFUL BUTTERFLIES

*There's nothing quite so summery as the sight
of a brightly-coloured butterfly visiting
the flowers on a hot, windless day.
All River Bankers know these handsome insects well,
so here's a chance for you to find out more about
them. (There are more on pages 32 and 58, too!)*

THE SWALLOWTAIL

To see the beautiful Swallowtail you'd have to go to the Norfolk Broads, because that's the only part of the country in which it lives. At one time, it was to be seen all over East Anglia and down as far as the Thames marshes, but unhappily it died out.

The Swallowtail feeds on only one type of plant, and that is the Milk Parsley. The young caterpillars are black with a white stripe, but after they shed their skins for the second time they become totally different, changing to bright green with black and orange rings.

The butterflies emerge from the pupa (that's the stage the caterpillars go into during Autumn, for over-Wintering) from late May until mid-July.

Entomologists, that's the name for people who study insects, and lepidopterists, who study butterflies and moths in particular, are trying to re-establish colonies of the Swallowtail in other parts of Eastern England.

DID YOU KNOW...

. . . that the Swallowtail is the largest British butterfly? Females can have a wingspan of up to 100mm (4in). The smallest British butterfly is the Small Blue, with a wingspan of between 19 and 25mm (¾ and 1in).

. . . that the Anglo-Saxons called the Brimstone butterfly, one of the first to appear in the Spring, Buttorfleoge, because it was the colour of butter? Their word may have become used, over the years, to mean *all* butterflies.

. . . that people often believe butterflies live only for a day? This is a myth, as many of them survive for up to a year.

Ah, yes! Well, these two pictur
look the same, don't they? But
actually, seven changes have
been made to the second one.
Can you spot them?

ot in front of
iissing.
bow tie
from red to
. Moley's
s missing,
loaf of bread
ie picnic basket.

A CHANGE!

The change
1. Leaves missing
the middle bran
the top of the pi
2. Second wi
from left c
cottage mis
3. Handrail on
changed from gr

WAYFARERS ALL

Autumn had arrived. As August left and the first winds of September rustled the trees, the world seemed to shake itself out of its snooze and grow restless.

He couldn't say why, but deep down in his bones, the Water Rat felt oddly discontented. He stood on the edge of the river outside his house, and heard the impatient clatter of wings as a skein of geese flew overhead, and he shifted uneasily from foot to foot.

"Bother," he said. "Oh, piffle." And with his hands thrust deep into his pockets, he wandered inland.

He soon came upon the Fieldmice and Harvest Mice, friends who usually had a spare moment to gossip and exchange news with a visitor. But today they were busy.

Some were hauling out dusty trunks and dress baskets. Others were sorting out their belongings, and one or two were eagerly poring over maps and plans.

"What do you think of this for a desirable residence?" said one. "Not too far away, is it?"

"Not at all," agreed another. "Quite convenient, really."

The Rat said: "Look here, you fellows! What are you up to?"

"It's Ratty," said one of them with a hasty smile.

"It isn't time to be thinking of Winter quarters yet," said the Rat, as someone nudged him out of the way. "Not by a long chalk."

"Oh yes, we know," said a Fieldmouse. "But it's always as well to be in good time. We want to get all our furniture and baggage and stores moved out before those horrid machines come clicking round the fields."

"But it's a splendid day," protested the Rat. "Come for a stroll along the hedge."

"Well, I think — not today, thank you, Mr. Rat," said one of them. And "Maybe when we've more time,"

"Come for a stroll along the hedge."

"Well, I think — not today, thank you, Mr. Rat."

"Maybe when we've more time."

added another.

"Bosh!" snorted the Rat. "Bother all of you with your stupid packing and fuss!"

He turned away sharply, and fell over a hatbox at his feet. With another snort of annoyance, he picked himself up, and immediately fell over something else.

"If some people would be more careful," he began, but one of the Fieldmice interrupted, picking up his spilled belongings. "If some people would look where they're going," he said acidly, "they wouldn't hurt themselves!"

Sighing, the Rat returned to his faithful, steady-going old river, which never packed up, stowed anything away, nor went into Winter quarters. High above, there was a twittering of swallows, but here was the chummy Otter, and his full-of-beans son, Portly.

"Otter! I'm so glad to see you," said the Rat. "At least you're not going anywhere. Just look at those chattering birds! It's much too early. I call it simply ridiculous."

"Oh," said the Otter. "They're not off yet. Just making plans, you know, and deciding which route to take, and where to stop on the way. They say that's half the fun."

"Fun?" shrugged the Rat. "I don't understand." Then his face broke into a smile as he saw Portly scramble out of the water and shake his fur on the bank.

"Did you see my dive, Mr. Rat? That was one of my best ones!"

"Now then, Portly," said Otter. "No boasting."

Rat chuckled. "Suppose we go for a saunter somewhere. Down towards the weir, perhaps?"

Otter whistled and shook his head. "Sorry, old chap. Too busy. Winter coming. The river will soon be running high. Portly has to learn to swim against the current. . ."

The Rat sighed as his friends turned away and got on with their urgent business. "Maybe the Mole will fancy coming for a picnic," he said to himself.

But it was the same story. As the Rat suggested it, the Mole made apologetic noises. "I was thinking of

"Why is everyone so concerned about Winter on a lovely sunny day like this? Why can't people stay put and be jolly?"

"You know how it is, Ratty, you get a feeling in your bones that it's time to do something, and then off you go and do it."

15

going to Mole End," he said, hesitantly.

"Whatever for?" exclaimed the Rat.

"Well, the usual thing, you know. Getting it ready for Winter."

The Rat threw up his hands in despair. "Why **is** everyone so concerned about Winter on a lovely sunny day like this? Why can't people stay put and be jolly?"

"You know how it is, Ratty," said the Mole. "You get a feeling in your bones that it's time to do something, and then off you go and do it. Of course, if you really want to stay and have a picnic, I will. But. . ."

The Rat looked at him crossly as his friend carefully put away bathing costumes and sunglasses and sandals into a large carpet bag. "Don't bother if you don't feel like it," he said, peevishly. "If you want to clear off like everyone else, jolly well go and do it. See if I care!"

Moley felt hurt, but there was no use arguing with the Rat, and so he shuffled away with his bag. He didn't understand that the Rat was hearing the same restless call without knowing what it was.

Long after the Mole had gone, Ratty was sitting outside his home with his hands clasped around his knees, when along the towpath a figure came in sight. A grey figure, wearing a knitted jersey of faded blue, his breeches patched and stained, some belongings tied up in a blue cotton handkerchief. It was the Wayfarer Rat, and he was singing a haunting sort of song to himself.

The Water Rat raised his head as the first strains of the song came to him. He stood up, slowly, interested.

"Good day, friend," said the Wayfarer Rat, drawing abreast.

"Hullo," said the Water Rat, amiably. "Won't you — er — sit down and rest awhile?"

The Wayfarer Rat nodded, shrugged off his bundle, and sprawled on the grass. "There's a whiff of clover on the wind," he said. "Behind the sharp smell of the river." Then, seeming to study Ratty for a while, "I see you're a freshwater sailor. It's a goodly life you lead, friend."

"It's **the** life," said the Water Rat. "The **only** life." Yet somehow, he didn't sound, even to himself, as convincing as he usually was.

17

"I'm a seafaring rat, myself," said the Wayfarer. "I come from a far-off port called Constantinople."

Ratty licked his lips, and when his voice came, it was an enchanted whisper. "Constantinople!" he breathed.

"Aye, matey," said the Wayfarer. "The Levant. The Grecian Isles. The golden days and the warm, balmy nights. Sleeping in some cool temple or ruined cistern, feasting and song after sundown, under the great stars in a velvet sky. In and out of harbour all the time, old friends everywhere until at last you ride down to Venice on a ribbon of moonlit gold!"

The Water Rat sat entranced, his mouth open wide, as his companion painted word-pictures of magical cities and glittering harbours. Of tall ships and wondrous-smelling cargoes. Of barbary pirates and rats with rings in their ears. Of lamp-lit taverns on distant quays, and parched olive-groves, and places where food and drink were there for the taking.

Then he found his manners.

"Talking of food," said the Water Rat, "will you stay and eat with me?"

"Thank 'ee," said the Wayfarer. "I must say I don't mind if I do."

While they dined, the Wayfarer continued to cast the spell of far-away places. The Water Rat heard of Rhodes, and Athens, and Egypt, and all the thrill of voyages over every one of the Seven Seas, and at last he began to understand the longing that stirred deep inside him. His eyes were glazed and far-away when, eventually, his visitor shook himself to his feet.

"Well, I must be off on the road again," said the Wayfarer. "Until I reach the little sea town I know so well. There, sooner or later, the ships of all seafaring nations arrive, and there, at the destined hour, the ship of my choice will let go its anchor. . .

"Let go its anchor. . !" repeated the enthralled Water Rat, in a whisper.

The Wayfarer's eyes twinkled. "And you'll come too, my friend," he said. "For the days pass, and the South still calls. And it waits for you. . ."

"It does. . ?" Poor Ratty was still lost in some kind

"Well, I must be off on the road
again, until I reach the little
sea town I know so well. There, sooner or
later, the ships of all seafaring nations
arrive, and there, at the destined hour,
the ship of my choice will
let go its anchor. . ."

"Let go its anchor. . ."

19

of dream.

"Aye. Take adventure. Heed the call. 'Tis but a banging on the door behind you. Out of the old life, and into the new!"

Singing his song again, the Wayfarer strode off down the river, and Ratty watched him go.

Then, like a sleepwalker, the Water Rat turned and began to pack food and clothes into a satchel. Over and over, he whispered one word to himself. "Constantinople". . .

It was the Otter who saw the Water Rat walk past. "Hey, Ratty! Where are you going?" But there was no reply.

"Hmmph. Must be thinking up one of his poems," muttered Otter, and turned back to giving Portly his swimming lessons.

The Mole, however, had been worried about his friend, and having done as much as he could to make Mole End neat and tidy, had gone back to Ratty's house to see if the Water Rat had come out of his irritable mood.

"Otter," cried Mole, spotting the animals in the river. "Have you seen Ratty?"

"Yes," said Otter. "He's just left."

"But where did he go?" said Mole.

"Down the road," shrugged Otter.

"He was very strange, Mr. Mole," added Portly. "He never said 'hullo, Portly'. And he **always** says 'hullo, Portly'."

"Portly's quite right," said Otter. "In fact, the only thing he **did** say was — 'Constantinople'."

Now Mole was really worried. On his way back to Mole End, he'd seen the Wayfarer Rat, and had known what he was. He ran as fast as his legs could carry him, and tugged at the bell outside the Badger's front door. "Oh my, oh my!" he said to himself. "Ratty's been and gone and done something silly! Mr Badger will know what to do!"

But a cheeky weasel reminded Mole that Badger had gone to sleep for the Winter, and wouldn't take kindly to being disturbed, so the Mole had to think again!

"Otter! Have you seen Ratty?"

"Yes, he's just left."

"He was very strange, Mr. Mole.
He never said 'hullo, Portly'.
And he always says 'hullo, Portly'."

"Toady! That's it!" He ran, puffing, all the way to Toad Hall, and just as he had expected, the Toad was delighted to see him!

"Come in, dear chap! Some tea! I have excellent crumpets, all the way from London! Some world-renowned madeira cake. . ."

"Do stop, Toady," pleaded Mole. "I need your help!"

"Oh! You **do**?" The Toad swelled with pride. "Tell me, my good fellow!"

"It's Ratty," gasped the Mole. "He's left home, and I'm sure he's in some kind of trouble. I think he's gone off with a seafarer Rat!"

"Splendid!" exclaimed Toad. "I shall look up seafarer rats in my leather-bound, gold-blocked encyclopedias, and. . ."

"No, no," interrupted the Mole. "What we have to do is **follow** them!"

"Oh, even better!" beamed Toad. "In that case, we shall use my latest car!"

"Oh, I'm not so sure about that," said the dismayed Mole, but there was no stopping Toad! In the twinkling of an eye, he threw on his cap and goggles, and within minutes the two animals were on their way down the drive of Toad Hall!

"Poop-poop!" chortled Toad, blowing the horn. "We'll find them in no time!"

After a while, Mole found his voice.

"I think it's got something to do with going South," he said.

"South?" boomed Toad. "Capital! My Grandfather always went there. Monte Carlo, you know. Gambling, champagne. . ."

"That doesn't sound much like Ratty," said the Mole. And then, seeing a horse leaning over a gate, "Stop, Toady! Stop!"

The car came to an uncertain stop.

"I say, Horse, you haven't seen a rat passing this way by any chance?" asked the Mole.

"No," agreed the Horse. "I haven't. But I have seen **two** rats."

"Dash it all," put in the impatient Toad. "In that case, where does this road lead to?"

"Are you asking me?" said the Horse.

"Yes I **am**, my good nag," said Toad, irritably.

"I am not your good nag, so you can go and jump in the lake," said the Horse, and it took the Mole a good five minutes of cajoling and wheedling and not a little bit of flattery to get him to change his mind.

"All right," said the Horse, grudgingly. "It goes to the Sea."

"We're on the right track," whooped Toad, delightedly. "Hang on, Mole, old chap! Poop-Poop!" And off they went again.

What the Horse hadn't told them was that it was a rather **long** road. And soon, darkness began to fall. It was clear that Toad would have to stop and put his lights on, and that was far from being an easy business.

Toad's car-lights were old-fashioned acetylene ones, and lighting them made him burn his fingers, and sulk, and insist that lights weren't really necessary at all.

"I have double vision," he told the Mole.

"I'm not surprised," said the Mole. "But that doesn't make it any better."

"Of course it does," said Toad. "Double vision means a chap can see twice as well!"

Fretting, because he knew that time was running out, Mole kept Toad at it, and though Toad kept burning his fingers even more the lamps were eventually lit, and they continued their journey.

At last, they came over a rise and saw the lights of the harbour town far in the distance.

"Is that it, Toady?" asked Mole.

The Toad stood up, removed his goggles, and peered under his hand. "I can see ships' masts against the clouds," he said. "And lanterns. Green and red and white."

"Are any of them moving?"

"No," said the Toad. "At least, I don't think so. I say, you know I've never seen such ships before, but they sail East, and West, and South and North — oh — everywhere! What fun!"

"But suppose Ratty's already on one of them," wailed the Mole. "Oh, do hurry up, Toady! We mustn't be too late!"

"I have double vision."

"I'm not surprised. But that doesn't make it any better."

"Of course, it does. Double vision means a chap can see twice as well!"

Meanwhile, down by the dockside, in the yellow glow of a swinging lamp, the Wayfarer Rat peered out of a ship's porthole and smiled. There, on the quay below him, he saw the uncertain figure of the Water Rat.

"Ahhh! So you've come, my river friend," he said. "I knew you would! The ship sails at midnight, and you and I shall be messmates, all the way to the far Levant!"

As though in a trance, the Water Rat began to pace towards the ship's mooring rope. All he could see in his mind's eye were pictures of story-book countries and magical towns. He didn't hear the squeal of Toady's badly-applied brakes behind him, and never felt the clutch of the Mole's hand on his arm. . .

"Ratty! Wait!" yelled the Mole.

"Come **on**, matey," laughed the Wayfarer. "Ah, but the land tugs! There's always someone to cry when you go, but that's the seaman's life!"

"Help me, Toady! Help me!" wailed the Mole.

The Toad scampered forward and, slipping and sliding on the wet cobbles, lent his weight to assist the Mole in keeping the Water Rat from the rope.

The Water Rat struggled and fought, still like someone in a dream.

"Let me go! I have to go South with the rest of them! I see it all now! That longing for new places. . ! Oh, those distant, beguiling shores!"

Ratty! **Please!**" The Mole was almost beside himself. "You'd be lost, all alone on the oceans of the world!"

"Let me go, old chap!"

"We can't, Ratty! We **can't**!"

"This is your last chance," said the Wayfarer. "They're about to slip the moorings, matey. . ."

He began to sing his song again, and quite suddenly, even as the rope slipped from the bollard, the Water Rat burst into tears, and dropped like a limp bundle of washing to the quayside cobbles.

"Oh, Ratty," whimpered Moley, forlornly. "I **know** how you feel. . ."

Now the big ship was drawing away from the harbour, and the Wayfarer's song was fading on the wind. A seagull flew close and squawked wildly, as if to

destroy the spell, and the Mole and the Toad gently lifted their friend to his feet. . .

"We'll take him home now, Toady, please," said the Mole. . .

It was a long time before the Water Rat shook himself out of the silent gloom that had prevented him from saying a single word on the long journey back.

But now, in his own parlour, he wrung his hands and looked at his old friends with moist eyes.

"How can I explain to you the haunting sea voices, the magic of the Wayfarer, the magic and the dream. . ?"

"Don't try, old fellow," said Moley, kindly. He turned to Toad. "I'll look after him now."

"Oh," said Toad, a little disappointed. "Well, if you say so."

"You were splendid, Toady," said the Mole. "If it hadn't been for you we'd have lost Ratty for ever!"

Toad brightened. "Really? I **say!**"

The Mole heard him congratulating himself as he drove away, with many a boisterous 'poop-poop-poop'. He looked back at Ratty.

"You know, they're harvesting that field of wheat behind Mole End tomorrow, Ratty," he said. "You've never written any poems about the harvest, have you? About the harvest home, and all the jams, and apples, and cider they make. . ?"

"I don't believe I have," said the Rat, reaching for a pencil. "I believe you've given me inspiration, old chap!"

"I know I don't talk about things like Constantinople, and I'm a dull old chap really," muttered the Mole. "But. . ."

The Water Rat put out his hand and touched Mole on the arm. "You're the best of friends, dear old Moley, and I'm all right now, really I am. If you'd like to make a nice pot of tea. . ?"

"And some hot buttered toast?" said the Mole, his eyes glistening with happy tears.

"Hot buttered toast!" replied the Rat, with gusto. He put his feet up on the fender and sighed with peace. "Home, sweet Home ," he said. "When all's said and done, Moley, you can't beat it, you know!"

WHAT DO YOU KNOW ?

1. What are those poisonous toadstools, bright scarlet with white flecks, that you sometimes see in woods, called?

DEVIL'S DARNING-CONES
FLY AGARIC
SCARLET RUNNERS

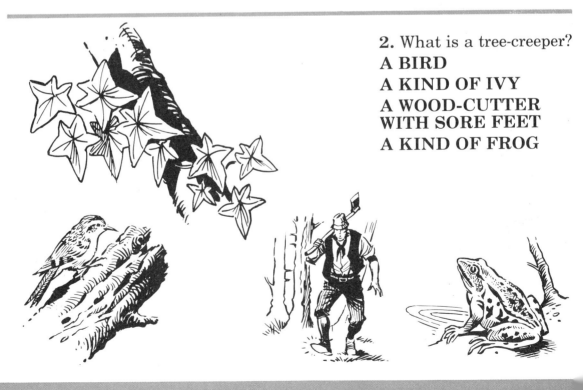

2. What is a tree-creeper?
A BIRD
A KIND OF IVY
A WOOD-CUTTER
WITH SORE FEET
A KIND OF FROG

All of us go out in the country sometimes, even if it's only to the local common. Well, how wide-open do you keep your eyes? See if you can answer these questions about the things you stand a chance of seeing whenever you're out of town...

3. Acorns, cob-nuts and conkers come from three different trees. Which ones, from the following list?

ELM
HOLLY
OAK
BEECH
HORSE-CHESTNUT
HAZEL

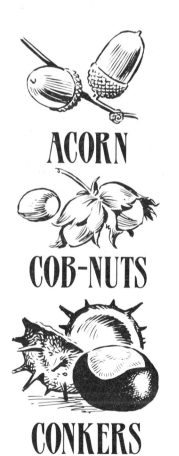

ACORN

COB-NUTS

CONKERS

4. In country talk, what is a 'Yaffle'?

A KIND
OF FARM
IMPLEMENT

A WOODPECKER

A 'FOREIGNER'
FROM ANOTHER
VILLAGE

1. Fly-Agaric. 2. A bird. 3. Acorn from Oak, Cob-nut from Hazel, Conker from Horse-Chestnut. 4. A woodpecker, because its call is like a yaffling laugh.

ANSWERS

BEAUTIFUL BUTTERFLIES

THE PEACOCK

Anyone can see how these beautiful butterflies got their name: the markings on their wings look just like the markings you find on a peacock's tail-feathers.

The 'eyes', as they are known, on a Peacock butterfly's wings are actually a kind of defensive protection. Many birds are partial to butterflies as a snack, and birds will often go for the 'eyes' first. So, as likely as not, the butterfly will escape attack with no more than a torn wing.

Caterpillars of the Peacock butterfly can be found on stinging nettles, which they like to eat. The butterflies themselves are one of those species that likes to spread their wings on a sunny path or a stone wall, so at least they are easy to see!

DID YOU KNOW...

. . . that many other butterflies have 'eye' markings on their wings to fool birds? Hedge Browns, Small Browns, Ringlets and Small Whites are among them.

. . . that the rarest British butterfly is the Large Tortoiseshell? It was officially declared extinct in 1979, although people keep claiming to have seen it in various parts of the country.

. . . that butterflies can fly at about six miles per hour? One species, though, the Monarch, which has been scientifically timed, can reach the amazing speed of 25mph!

. . . that male butterflies release complex scents to attract the females? These can sometimes be detected a fantastic six miles away! And often the scents resemble those of favourite feeding plants.

FARMYARD FUN

Well, there's plenty happening in this busy farmyard just along the Open Road and beyond the Wild Wood. But what's that in the middle, all dots and numbers? Join them up, starting at number 1, to find out! Now see how many things you can see in the picture that start with the letter B, and when you've done that, look for five deliberate mistakes that have been made in the drawing! Still keen? Take a look at the horses' names above the stable doors. They've been jumbled up, so see if you can unscramble them. After all that, why not try colouring the picture to make it nice and bright?

Stable signs: **LERRYMEGS**, **NIRCEP**, **BOBDIN**, **ROTTERT**, **ROVER**

ANSWERS

THE PIPER AT THE GATES OF DAWN

The midsummer day had been fiercely hot since sunrise.
What everybody looked for at such a time was a cool,
shady spot by the River, but such places were hard to
find, and many were well-kept secrets.

So somewhere in the undergrowth the deer would be
lying silently, birds would be still and quiet down
among the reeds or under their tree-top canopy, and the
loudest sound was the hum and buzz and drone of
insects who were too busy to mind the heat.

But for animals who were not river folk, animals
who lived underground, this kind of sweltering day was
very uncomfortable indeed. The Mole had tried to cool
his inside with ginger beer, and his outside with a wet
flannel, but neither seemed to make much difference.

The Water Rat, on the other hand, had gone fishing
with Otter and his little son, Portly, and to tell the truth,
the two older creatures had spent most of the day
drowsing.

"Amazing how sleepy one gets, just watching a float
bobbing, bobbing, bobbing," the Rat had murmured.

"Mmmm," agreed Otter. "Trouble is, they don't bob
half enough. The fish seem to be as lazy as we are."

Well, catching nothing is the best way to fish, as
any self-respecting fish will tell you, but young Portly
found it all rather dull. Time and again, he pulled in the
bent pin he'd tied to the end of a piece of string, sighed,
and dropped it back in the water. In a word, he was
bored.

Somewhere, a restless warbler trilled in the willows
nearby, and Portly put down his stick and wandered
away to see if he could catch sight of it.

"Don't you go too far, Portly," said Otter, looking at
him through half-closed eyes.

"*Don't you go too far, Portly.*"

Portly didn't see the warbler, which must have found singing a little too tiring, but he spotted a colourful butterfly, and followed it cautiously as it flitted from bush to bush down the river bank.

At last, the Water Rat decided that it was time to pack up. With a long, sleepy sigh, he began to wind in his line, and Otter did the same.

"Portly," he said. And then, a little more loudly, "Portly?"

The youngster had disappeared beyond the screening willows, and Otter shook his head, smiling. "He would go wandering off at the last minute. Never mind. I'll soon find him. See you later, Ratty."

"Right-oh, old chap," said the Rat.

The Rat went into his living room to find the Mole sunk deep in an armchair. "Whew," he said, mopping his brow. "It's lovely and cool in here. I suppose we ought to think about supper, Moley."

"Well, how about some ginger beer while we think about it?" suggested the Mole.

"Capital idea! Be a good chap and fetch up a couple of bottles from the larder."

They were about to enjoy their drink when the Mole glanced out and saw Otter hurrying towards Ratty's home. "That's odd," he said. "He's looking worried."

Otter came straight in without knocking.

"Is Portly here, you fellows?" he said, anxiously.

The Rat shook his head.

"I've looked everywhere," said Otter.

"I thought perhaps he might have popped along to see Moley."

The Mole spread his hands. "I haven't seen him. Mind you, I've been dozing a bit, on and off, this afternoon, but if Portly had come here, I'm sure he'd have woken me. He's so fond of a ginger beer, is Portly."

The Otter was very anxious indeed, even though he tried to hide it. "He may have wandered inland," he said. "I'll go and ask around."

Ratty and Moley watched him go. "I hope the lad's all right," muttered the Rat. "His father thinks the world of him."

"I'm sure nothing's wrong," said the Mole. "You

know how Portly's always straying off and then turning up again. But no harm ever happens to him."

Suddenly, the Rat froze, and all the hairs on his neck began to prickle. Distantly, but coming ever nearer, there was the dismal sound of a hunting horn, and the baying of hounds!

"Quick, Mole! Hide!"

"But, but why? What is it?" said the Mole, alarmed.

"Back! Back! Don't make a sound!" The Rat was afraid, and his fear passed itself on to the Mole!

The dreadful noise came closer and closer! The whole of Ratty's house shook and shuddered as something terrible and monstrous swept along the river bank, unseen above them. Then, mercifully, it began to die away again into the distance.

"What, what **was** it, Ratty?" whispered the Mole.

"I've only heard it once before," said the Rat, grimly. "It was an Otter Hunt."

The Mole looked horrified. "You, you mean they want to harm **Otter**. . ?" He could hardly believe it.

The Rat's eyes were red with anger. "Otter will be all right," he said. "**He** knows how to get out of their way. . ."

The Mole gulped. "But — Portly. . ?" He hardly dared say it.

The two animals looked at each other, aghast!

Another blazing day had come, and was already on its way towards evening. From friends afar had come the welcome news that at least, the horrible Otter Hunt had not found a kill, and yet Portly was still missing.

Otter was far afield, searching still, and now the Badger had called a meeting of the others at Ratty's house. He cleared his throat and began.

"My friends, we all know why we are here. To find young Portly."

Toad puffed out his chest. "Excellent little fellow, Portly," he said. "So friendly and adventurous."

"Please don't interrupt, Toad," said the Badger, sharply. "Now, to continue. Everybody about here knows and likes that youngster, just as they do his father. Splendid chap, Otter. Very respectable, like his father before him.

41

"Our best hope is that if he has just wandered away and got lost, some animal or other will come across him and bring him home. At least we know no one round here would harm him. . ."

He turned to Toad. "Have you brought the map?"

The Toad produced it, and got himself thoroughly tied up trying to unfold it.

Badger sighed, and pointed at a spot on the map. "Portly was last seen here," he said. "Now, assuming that our information is correct, and that he escaped. . . that he was not, **harrumph**, well **you** know. . . He could be anywhere from here. To here."

He paused and looked round. "I suggest that the four of us cover this area, asking all the animals we meet whether they have seen the child."

Rat said: "If I take the boat and row upriver. . ."

"I'll drive my car along the road," interrupted Toad. But he was instantly hushed by the Badger.

"No, Toad. You will **walk**. Downriver." "But, Badger," wailed Toad. "I could cover more ground in my motor car!"

Sternly, Badger said: "That may be, but you would not be able to question many animals when you were upside down in a ditch."

"I **say**!" said the Toad, offended. He looked at Ratty and the Mole for support, but there was none. "Oh, all right," he muttered at last.

"That's settled, then," said the Badger. "Mole, you will cover the area round Mole End, and I myself will search the Wild Wood."

"The Wild Wood!" exclaimed the Rat. "That would take days!"

Perhaps you'd like me to help," suggested the Mole, nervously. And the Rat looked at him admiringly, knowing how much the Wild Wood terrified his friend.

Badger smiled. "No thank you, Mole. It **is** a large area, but I must just do the best I can."

At that moment, they all turned, for there was a hoarse cough behind them, and there stood none other than The Chief Weasel!

"'Ullo, Mr. Badger."

Toad bristled at the sight of his old enemy. "What are

"'Ullo, Mr. Badger."

"What are you doing here?"

you doing here?" he snorted. "How did you get in?"

The Chief Weasel ignored him. "We heard you were looking for young Portly, Mr. Badger," he said.

"What of it?" blared Toad, fairly hopping with indignation.

"Shut up, Toady," said the Rat.

The weasel continued. "Nice little chap, that Portly. No side about him. Often used to pop up in the woods. I've got a nipper myself, and him and young Portly used to have a bit of a game together. You'd never think he was, well, one of the nobs. So, if we can do anything to help, I just thought. . ."

"You think we'd accept help from weasels?" scoffed Toad. He was instantly silenced by the Badger.

"Besides, Mr. Badger," went on the Chief Weasel, you done me a favour once. I said I'd pay you back one day, and if you, that is to say, if. . ."

Badger nodded gravely. "We shall be honoured to accept your assistance," he said.

And so, from the River Bank to the Wild Wood, the search for Portly began in earnest.

Upstream, the Water Rat questioned a group of fieldmice, but none of them had seen the little Otter.

Near Mole End, the Mole had words with a more-than-prickly hedgehog, but he, too, knew nothing of the little fellow's disappearance.

And Toad? Downriver, he'd found nobody at all.

Unlikely allies, the Badger and the Chief Weasel's men combed the Wild Wood. They, too, learned nothing to help them.

It was a gloomy gathering that met again that night in Ratty's house.

Toad, good soul that he really was, had arranged for a splendid supper for them all to be brought over from Toad Hall, but few felt like eating. The Chief Weasel's assistant, however, didn't like to see good grub going begging, and reached for a cake. He got his fingers rapped by his boss for his pains.

"No, no," said the Toad, swallowing his dislike of weasels as he felt Badger's eye on him. "**Do** have one!"

Then, his shoulders bowed, the Otter came in.

"Portly. . ?" The Rat was first with the question, but

the gloomy Otter shook his head.

"No sign of him anywhere. I'm at the end of my tether."

"Dear old Otter," said Toad, kindly. "Have a hot drink, and a sandwich. There are some sardine ones there. You'll like those."

The Otter hardly heard him. "I'm going back to that place where we were fishing, Ratty," he said. "That was the spot where I taught him to swim. He loves it there. If he **does** come back, that's where he'll be."

The Badger looked very doubtful indeed. "But Otter, my dear chap," he began. . .

Otter still wasn't listening. "I think I'll wait there tonight. On the off chance, you know. Just on the off chance."

"There's nothing more we can do tonight," said the Badger as Otter left. "And by the way, you weasels have done nobly."

"Oh, thank you, Mr. Badger," beamed the Assistant Chief Weasel, holding his hand out for a tip. Very properly, his boss slapped it, outraged.

The Chief Weasel said: "We'll start the search again at first light, Mr. Badger."

"Don't we get anyfing?" hissed his assistant as the Chief Weasel hustled him out of the house.

"Ain't you ever heard of nobbles oblige?" said the Chief, irritably.

"What's that, then? Worth a few quid is it?"

"Never mind!" barked his boss, who really hadn't the faintest idea himself what his curious phrase meant. He covered up his confusion by kicking his assistant in the pants!

Left alone, the four friends looked at each other. All of them were trying hard not to yawn. It had been a hard and unrewarding day.

"You fellows had better get some sleep," said the Badger. "I might catch forty winks myself."

"Badger, we can't just go to bed," said the Mole. "Not while poor little Portly. . ."

The Badger shook his head solemnly.

"If he's still alive," he said. "Which I very much doubt. . ."

"You fellows had better get some sleep. I might catch forty winks myself."

"Badger, we can't just go to bed. Not while poor little Portly. . ."

47

"Badger! Don't say that!" exclaimed the Rat in horror.

Badger shrugged. "If he was frightened by that hunt and just ran away and got lost," he said, "then he'll be tired out by now, and curled up somewhere to sleep. We'll begin again at first light."

He made his way back to his own home, a lantern in his hand. At the door, he paused, and raised the lamp so that its light flickered on the bushes. "Portly. . !" he called hopefully. There was no answer, and the Badger, with a heavy-hearted sigh, went inside.

Deeper in the Wild Wood, the Chief Weasel and his assistant were approaching the Weasel Den.

"Time to turn in now, gov'nor?"

"Mmm?" The Chief Weasel clubbed at some bushes as though he bore them a grudge. "No," he grumbled, anxious in case his henchman thought him 'soft'. "I — er — I reckon I'll sit down out here for a bit. Just in case, like. Well, it's a bit warm to go in, just yet."

Tired though they were, Otter's friends couldn't sleep at all. Long past midnight, Toad came to the door of Toad Hall in his dressing gown and peered out into the darkness.

"I say, Portly old chap," he quavered, "you're not there, are you? Portly. . ?"

At the Water Rat's home, the Rat and the Mole had spent ages wasting time in putting things away and pretending to make ready to go to bed. At last, Mole gave up the pretence.

"It's no use, Ratty. I simply can't go and turn in, and go to sleep and do nothing, even though there doesn't seem to be anything left to do!"

"Just what I was thinking myself," said the Rat. "Why don't we get the boat out and paddle upstream?"

"Oh, Ratty! **Could** we?" The Mole rubbed his paws together.

"We can search as well as we can," said the Rat.

By the light of the moon, the two friends got out the boat, and while Mole sat looking anxiously from side to side, the Rat rowed slowly up-river.

Dark as it was, and deserted, the river was full of small noises. The chatter and rustling of the busy little

population who were up and about all night. Despite the anxious nature of their search, the Mole and the Rat felt a strange sense of peace.

"There's a backwater over there, Ratty," said the Mole at length. "Shall we try up there?" The Rat nodded and pulled more strongly on one of the oars so that the boat's nose turned towards the deeply-hung reach of still, black water. . .

Moments earlier, both of them had heard the uncertain notes of a bird, waking just too early for the dawn chorus. But now, in this dark and mysterious reach of the river, a total silence came down. A deep and thrilling silence as though all the world was waiting for something, it knew not what.

"There's an island here, Ratty," whispered the Mole. "I don't remember seeing it before."

"No. We never come here. I don't quite know why," said the Rat, whispering too. He rested on his oars, and his nostrils were quivering. A tingling ran up and down his spine.

"Do — do you hear something now, Mole?"

The Mole shook his head. "Only the wind in the reeds, Ratty."

"No! It — it was something else!" The Rat sat stock still. "There! Surely you can hear it now. . ?"

Softly, oh, so softly, but now growing stronger and stronger, the bubbling notes of the Pan Pipes. A haunting, lingering, spell-binding melody that struck deep into the Mole's heart and sent it wildly beating! Enthralled, he leaned forward.

"Oh, yes, Ratty! I hear it now! Follow it! We **must** follow it!"

As in a dream, while the liquid music flowed over them, around them, as if it came from all sides, the Rat and the Mole tied up their boat and crept softly through the carpet of wild flowers that spread over the island's shores.

And now there came the song. Words that they felt, more than heard.

"Lest the awe should dwell,
And turn your frolic to fret,

You shall look on my power at the helping hour,
But then you shall forget. . ."

"Ratty, I'm afraid," whispered the Mole.
"No! Not afraid," said the Rat. "Something else, but not — afraid! Come on!" He reached for his friend's paw, and they heard again the mystic words of the song. . .

"Lest limbs be reddened and rent,
I spring the trap that is set.
As I loose the snare, you may glimpse me there,
But then you shall forget!"

"What does it mean, Ratty?" Mole whispered.
"I don't know, Moley! I don't know!"
Now, in the first light of dawn, they came upon the clearing. And yet, it was as though light itself came from the statue that stood there. The old stone statue of the god, Pan.
With massive, curving horns, the pipes lowered from the broad, smiling mouth, it looked down on them gently, and again, even as the two animals put their paws up to cover their eyes in awe, came the song. . .

"Helper and healer, I cheer
Small waifs in the woodland wet.
Strays I find in it, wounds I bind in it,
Bidding them then forget. . . forget. . . forget. . ."
Now the sun had risen, and at once, both music and song faded fitfully, to blend with the chorus of bird-song that must surely have been going on all the time.
Slowly, the Rat and the Mole lowered their arms.
"What — what was it, Ratty?"
The Rat shook his head. "I don't know. I just felt it was meant for us. I've heard that there's something, or someone who looks after animals in trouble, Mole. It said — I **think** it said — **forget**. . ?"
Suddenly, the Rat gripped his friend's arm and pointed down between the cloven hooves of the statue! A small creature lay curled up there, blissfully asleep!
"It's Portly!" shouted the Rat!

"What — what was it, Ratty?"

"I don't know. I just felt it was meant for us. I've heard that there's something, or someone, who looks after animals in trouble, Mole. It said — I think it said — forget. . ?"

Mole gasped. "Just lying there, as safe and sound as if he was in his father's arms! Well, did you ever!"

"Portly? Portly! Wake up, young feller-me-lad!" said Rat, shaking the youngster's shoulder.

"Mr. Rat! Mr. Mole!" Portly sat up, rubbed the sleep from his eyes, and beamed at them. Then a frown stole across his little face.

"Where is he?"

"Who, Portly?" said the Rat.

Portly looked up at the statue. "I got lost," he said. "And then there was an awful noise, and I was afraid, and I ran away!" He rubbed his eyes. "**He** came. He — and — oh, my! I **forget**!"

The young otter began to cry, and ran this way and that, as though looking for something, or someone. . .

"You've been dreaming, old chap," said the Rat, kindly. "Come on, now. Your father's going to be terribly pleased to see you. . ."

Little Portly cheered up, and together, the three animals left the clearing. They didn't look back, but had they done so, they would have sworn there was an even broader smile on the face of the strange old statue. A faint flutter of pan-pipe music mingled triumphantly with the chorus of the birds. . .

The moment Otter saw Portly, he rushed forward and gathered his son up in his arms, hugging him close. The Rat and the Mole could see the tears of joy in his eyes, and Ratty tugged out his handkerchief and blew his nose, loudly. "Er, let's go and spread the good news," he said, gruffly.

Later, in the Water Rat's home, the Rat and the Mole sprawled out in their chairs, tired but happy.

"Was it a dream, Ratty?" said the Mole.

"Perhaps. But not quite," said the Rat, softly. "I say, Mole, it's pleasant to lounge here, listening to the wind, far off in the reeds. . ."

And the wind in the reeds made the music that they'd heard, but had forgotten, as the great healer and helper had said they would. And though strange memories would from time to time return, neither the Rat nor the Mole would know that they had come face to face with the Piper At The Gates Of Dawn. . .

"Er, let's go and spread the good news."

IN A WORD...

ALL CHANGE

Can you change TOAD to HALL, changing only one letter at a time, in only four moves?

TOAD

TOAD
LOAL
L

HALL

ACROSS

1. There's wind in these! (7)
5. When driving, Toad ought to do this when the lights are red! (4)
6. Rabbits have long ones. (4)
7. Respectful young animals call Toad this. (3)
9. Ratty has a paw at the end of this! (3)
10. A mischief-maker. (3)
11. Tiny. (3)
13. Something that Toad always seems to have lots of! (4)
14. ---- Seaman, a seafarer. (4)
15. Weasels and their kind break into places and steal things. This is what they are! (7)

DOWN

1. What you get when the river drops over a cliff. (9)
2. All animals, **and** you, speak through these! (4)
3. Opposite of 'under', it's also something you have in cricket. (4)
4. Moley does this when he's getting up the bank, having fallen in the river. (9)
8. Another word for rage. (3)
11. Owl call, coming after 'Tu-whit-tu. . .' (4)
12. After a long and busy day, Ratty and Moley put their feet up and take their ----. (4)

WORD SEARCH

All the words in the list below can be found in this square by simply searching them out, reading in straight lines. But those straight lines can go in any direction: up, down, backwards, forwards or diagonally. You don't need to use every letter in the square and you can use any of them more than once if you like. When you've used up all your spaces, you should be left with sixteen unused letters. If you put them all together and unscramble them, you'll be left with a very familiar book title!

CRACK THE CODE

If A = 1, B = 2, C = 3, and so on through the alphabet until Z = 26, can you decode this pair of words? They're very important indeed to *The Wind In The Willows*!

11 5 14 14 5 20 8
7 18 1 8 1 13 5

RIDDLE-ME-REE

What did King Neptune say when the sea dried up?
I haven't a notion! (an ocean)

What sort of things always get into the papers?
Fish and chips!

What did the pony say when he coughed?
Excuse me, I'm just a little hoarse!

What keeps the Sun up in the sky?
Sun-beams!

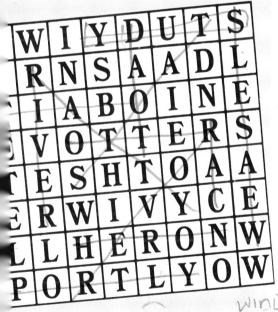

W	I	Y	D	U	T	S	
R	N	S	A	A	D	L	L
I	A	B	O	I	N	E	E
V	O	T	T	E	R	S	S
E	S	H	T	O	A	A	A
R	W	I	V	Y	C	E
L	L	H	E	R	O	N	W
P	O	R	T	L	Y	O	W

STUDY   OTTER
LATE   ROVER
RATTY   CAR
TOAD   HERON
STOAT   PORTLY
WEASELS   BAIT
    RIVER

[handwritten: WIND IN THE WILLOWS / TEL / OWAHGTSDIA OWLL]

ANSWERS

BEAUTIFUL BUTTERFLIES

THE PAINTED LADY

The Painted Lady is a migrant to these shores: it comes to Britain from North Africa usually in April or May. You can see this butterfly making its zig-zag course over dry fields and meadows, looking for food. Nobody knows the reason for its long journey, but whole colonies of migratory butterflies have been seen far out over the sea, like a moving, colourful cloud.

As with certain species of birds, the butterflies gather in their thousands at their own chosen 'airfield', and at some unseen and unknown signal, they all take off together, assemble in a formation, perhaps a mile wide, and then head whichever way they are compelled to go by their instinct.

DID YOU KNOW...

. . . that if you want to attract butterflies to your garden, you should plant the shrub Buddleia and the easily-grown Sedum, with its fleshy leaves? Better forget about nettles, though, so beloved of many caterpillars!

. . . that the Red Admiral, another migrating butterfly, is not so-called because of its sea-going habit? The word is a corruption of 'admirable', which indeed describes these handsome insects.

. . . that seventy species of butterfly are termed 'British', but only fifty-nine of them breed in this country?

. . . that caterpillars are rather greedy? Compared with the human scale, if the caterpillar of a Monarch butterfly was a six pound baby, the amount of food it ate would make it weigh eight tons in two weeks!

TRY YOUR LUCK

1 This river has far too many backwaters! Can you help the fish swim out to the lake!

2 Can you unscramble this jumbled picture and name the eight things that are all absolutely essential to a jolly good picnic?

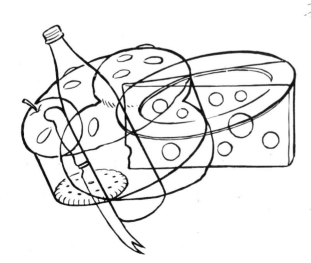

3 Bet you've never seen an animal like **this** before! Actually, it's a creature made up from parts of four normal creatures. Can you name them?

Have a go at these puzzles and see if you can solve them. See how quickly you can get the answers!

4

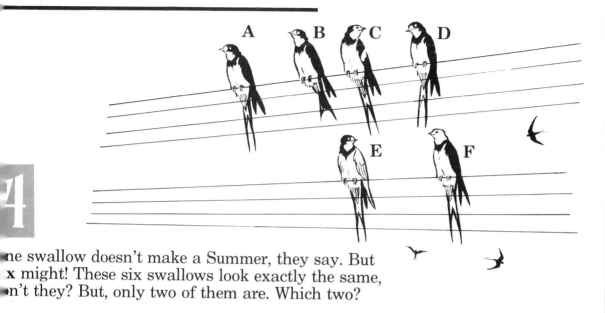

ne swallow doesn't make a Summer, they say. But
x might! These six swallows look exactly the same,
n't they? But, only two of them are. Which two?

5

Only one of these ropes ties the
rowing-boat to the tree on the
bank. Which one is it?

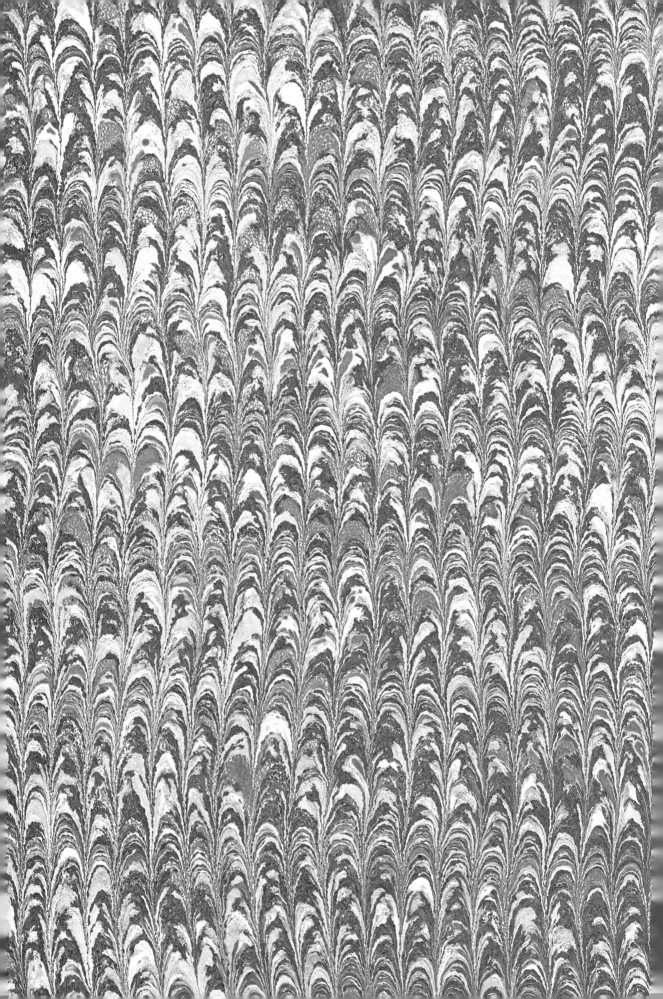